Howard Glyndon

Idyls of Battle and Poems of the Rebellion

Howard Glyndon

Idyls of Battle and Poems of the Rebellion

ISBN/EAN: 9783337210335

Printed in Europe, USA, Canada, Australia, Japan

Cover: Foto ©Andreas Hilbeck / pixelio.de

More available books at **www.hansebooks.com**

IDYLS OF BATTLE

AND

POEMS OF THE REBELLION.

By HOWARD GLYNDON.

(LAURA C. REDDEN.)

God! how this land grows rich in loyal blood
  Poured out upon it to its utmost length;
The incense of a nation's sacrifice —
  The wrested offering of a nation's strength!

It is the costliest land beneath the sun!
  'T is priceless, purchaseless! And not a rood
But hath its title written clear, and signed
  In some slain hero's consecrated blood!

NEW YORK:

PUBLISHED BY HURD AND HOUGHTON,

401 BROADWAY, COR. WALKER ST.

1865.

RIVERSIDE, CAMBRIDGE:

STEREOTYPED AND PRINTED BY

H. O. HOUGHTON AND COMPANY.

TO ONE

WHOSE QUIET WORDS OF PRAISE WOULD MAKE ME PROUD-
EST OF ALL; BUT WHOSE NAME IS TOO SACRED TO
BE WRITTEN UPON THIS PAGE:

WHO WAS TO MY PAST, IN THE HIGHEST SENSE
OF THE WORDS,

FRIEND AND COUNSELLOR,

AND WHOSE PRESENCE IN THE HEREAFTER WILL BE
DEAREST TO ME, AFTER GOD'S,

I consecrate this,

MY FIRST ENDEAVOR.

Shall not the earnest spirit plead for the untried hand?

CONTENTS.

PREFACE TO SUBSCRIBERS' EDITION.

———

TO the gentlemen whose names follow these lines I owe most cordial and grateful acknowledgments for friendly encouragement and active coöperation with me in the work of getting out this volume. One and all, they have my most fervent thanks.

Hon. A. LINCOLN, President U. S.

U. S. GRANT, Lieut.-General U. S.

Hon. J. A. GRISWOLD, M. C., Troy, New York.

H. D. BACON, Esq., St. Louis, Missouri.

Hon. H. T. BLOW, M. C., St. Louis, Missouri.

Hon. JOHN P. HALE, United States Senate, New Hampshire.

Hon. JOHN CONNESS, U. S. S., San Francisco, California.

Hon. TIMON O. HOWE, U. S. S., Wisconsin.

Maj.-Gen. L. H. ROUSSEAU, Army of the Ohio.

Hon. ROBERT C. SCHENCK, M. C., Ohio.

Hon. HENRY WILSON, U. S. S., Massachusetts.

Col. H. S. McCOMB, Wilmington, Delaware.

Ex-Gov. E. D. MORGAN, U. S. S., New York.

Hon. E. DELAFIELD SMITH, U. S. District Attorney, New York.

J. W. Parrish, Esq., St. Louis, Missouri.

Samuel Hallett, Esq., New York.*

Hon. Schuyler Colfax, M. C., Indiana.

Hon. John B. Steele, M. C., Kingston, New York.

John D. Perry, Esq., St. Louis, Missouri.

Hon. J. A. Garfield, M. C., Ohio.

Dr. W. K. Mehaffey, Washington, D. C.

Hon. J. A. Cravens, M. C., Hardensburgh, Indiana.

Hon. B. F. Loan, M. C., St. Joseph, Missouri.

Hon. J. W. McClurg, M. C., Linn Creek, Missouri.

Hon. B. Van Valkenburg, M. C., Bath, New York.

Hon. E. C. Ingersoll, M. C., Peoria, Illinois.

Hon. John G. Scott, M. C., Irondale, Missouri.

Hon. Wm. D. Kelley, M. C., Philadelphia, Pa.

Hon. J. A. J. Creswell, M. C., Elkton, Md.

Hon. Francisco Perea, Delegate from New Mexico.

Hon. Augustus Frank, M. C., New York.

Hon. Lucian Anderson, M. C., Mayfield, Ky.

Hon. E. H. Webster, M. C., Belair, Md.

Hon. Ben. Wood, M. C., New York City.

Hon. Thos. T. Davis, M. C., Syracuse, New York.

Ex-Gov. Wm. Sprague, U. S. S., Rhode Island.

Hon. Samuel Hooper, M. C., Boston, Mass.

Hon. Lewis W. Ross, M. C., Lewistown, Ill.

Hon. T. W. Kellogg, M. C., Grand Rapids, Michigan.

Hon. Green Clay Smith, M. C., Covington, Ky.

J. B. Stewart, Esq., Washington, D. C.

* Deceased.

Hon. NEHEMIAH PERRY, M. C., Newark, New Jersey.

Hon. C. H. WINFIELD, M. C., Goshen, New York.

Hon. H. P. BENNETT, Delegate from Colorado Territory.

Hon. J. F. FARNSWORTH, M. C., St. Charles, Ill.

Hon. J. A. JENKES, M. C., Providence, R. I.

Hon. N. B. SMITHERS, M. C., Dover, Delaware.

Hon. THOS. D. ELIOT, M. C., New Bedford, Mass.

Hon. H. C. DEMING, M. C., Hartford, Connecticut.

Hon. LEONARD MYERS, M. C., Philadelphia, Pa.

Hon. J. O'NEIL, M. C., Zanesville, Ohio.

Hon. W. B. ALLISON, M. C., Dubuque, Iowa.

Hon. WM. HIGBY, M. C., California.

Hon. CORNELIUS COLE, M. C., California.

Hon. M. F. ODELL, M. C., New York.

IN TIME OF WAR.

THERE are white faces in each sunny
    street,
  And signs of trouble meet us everywhere;
The nation's pulse hath an unsteady beat,
  For scents of battle foul the summer air.

A thrill goes through the city's busy life,
  And then — as when a strong man stints
    his breath —
A stillness comes; and each one in his place
  Waits for the news of triumph, loss, and
    death.

The " Extras " fall like rain upon a drought,
  And startled people crowd around the
    board

Whereon the nation's sum of loss or gain
  In rude and hurried characters is scored.

Perhaps it is a glorious triumph-gleam —
  An earnest of our Future's recompense ;
Perhaps it is a story of defeat,
  Which smiteth like a fatal pestilence.

But whether Failure darkens all the land,
  Or whether Victory sets its blood ablaze,
An awful cry, a mighty throb of pain,
  Shall scare the sweetness from these sum-
      mer days.

Young hearts shall bleed, and older hearts
      shall break,
  A sense of loss shall be in many a place ;
And oh, the bitter nights ! the weary days !
  The sharp desire for many a buried face !

God ! how this land grows rich in loyal
      blood,
  Poured out upon it to its utmost length !

The incense of a people's sacrifice, —
  The wrested offering of a people's strength!

It is the costliest land beneath the sun!
  'T is priceless, purchaseless! And not a
    rood
But hath its title written clear and signed
  In some slain hero's consecrated blood.

And not a flower that gems its mellowing
    soil
  But thriveth well beneath the holy dew
Of tears, that ease a nation's straining heart,
  When the Lord of battles smites it through
    and through.

LEFT ON THE BATTLE-FIELD.

OH, my darling! my darling! never to
    feel
  Your hand going over my hair!
Never to lie in your arms again, —
  Never to know where you are!
Oh, the weary miles that stretch between
  My feet and the battle-ground,
Where all that is left of my dearest hope
  Lies under some yellow mound!

It is but little I might have done
  To lighten your parting pain;
But 't is bitter to think that you died alone
  Out in the dark and the rain!
Oh, my hero love! — to have kissed the pain
  And the mist from your fading eyes!

To have saved one only passionate look
  To sweeten these memories!

And thinking of all, I am strangely stunned,
  And cannot believe you dead.
You loved me, dear! And I loved you,
    dear!
  And your letter lies there, unread!
You are not dead! You are not dead!
  God never could will it so —
To craze my brain and break my heart
  And shatter my life — I know!

Dead! dead! and never a word,
  Never a look for me!
Dead! dead! and our marriage-day
  Never on earth to be!
I am left alone, and the world is changed,
  So dress me in bridal white,
And lay me away in some quiet place
  Out of the hateful light.

TO THE EARNEST THINKERS.

IF the mist of failure, gray,
    Cloud the breaking of the day,
For whose coming all the waiting millions
      pray, —
    If misgivings dull and rust
    The first brightness of their trust, —
Let the earnest thinkers open up the way.

    Show each brave, impatient soul
    How the waves of failure roll
Back from brows that sternly front the wait-
      ing goal ;
    How the single-handed right,
    In its God-anointed might,
Dares to meet and conquer evil's legioned
      whole.

Show them how a brief defeat
Hath its uses pure and sweet, —
How it fires the brain, the soul, with newer
    heat ;
Failure's lowest depths we sound,
Then, with terrible rebound,
Up the heights of triumph go our conquering
    feet !

Show them how the Truth is strong
When it battles with the Wrong,
Though the coward quail before the struggle
    long ;
How the soldier of the Right
Dares the fierce, unequal fight,
Leaping fearless into Treason's armed throng !

Earnest thinkers of the day !
It is yours to clear the way,
While our soldiers fight, our women work
    and pray ;
Send your stirring words abroad
For the Right — for Truth — for God !
With the prophet's fiery spirit seal your say !

2

AFTER THE VICTORIES.

HA! the wine-press of pain hath been
  trodden!
And suffering's meed mantles high, —
The perfect, rare wine, wrought of patience,
  It moveth aright to the eye!
Oh! dark was the night while we trampled
  Its death-purple grapes under foot;
And no song parted silence from darkness,
  For Liberty's Sibyl was mute!

And the fiends of the lowest were loosened,
  To persecute Truth at their will!
They spat on her white shining forehead,
  She standing unmoved and still!
The hiss of the white-blooded coward,
  The vile breath of calumny's brood,
Befouled and bedarkened the kingdom,
  And poisoned the place where we stood!

We, — treading the ripe grapes asunder,
　With failing and overworked feet ;
Alone in the terrible darkness,
　Alone in the stifling heat ;
With agony-drops raining over
　Our weak hands from desolate brows ;
With a deadlier pain in our spirits,
　O'er whose failure no promise arose.

Shook the innermost being of justice,
　Stirred the innermost pulse of our God,
With a cry of remonstrance whose anguish
　Frighted devils and saints from its road !
All the pain of a long-martyred nation,
　All its giant heart's overtasked strength,
In one Samson-like throe were unfettered,
　Standing up for a hearing at length !

And, even as we fell in the darkness —
　Falling down, with our mouths in the dust,
With toil-stained and blood-dyed garments
　That betokened us true to our trust,
When the laugh of the scoffer was loudest,

And the clapping of cowardly hands,
   A glory blazed out from the Westward,
   That startled the far-distant lands !

     *   *   *   *   *   *

Ha ! the wine-press of pain hath been trodden!
   Now summon the laborers forth !
Let them come in their red-dyed garments,
   The lion-browed sons of the North !
Not for failure their veins have been leavened
   With the vintage of SEVENTY-SIX !
Nor unworthy the blood of our heroes
   With its rare olden currents to mix !

Ha ! Conquerors ! Come ye out boldly,
   Full fronting our reverent eyes !
In the might of your glorious manhood,
   Ye Saviours of Freedom, arise !
Come out in your sun-ripened grandeur,
   Ye victors, who wrestled with Wrong !
Come ! toil-worn and weary with battle, —
   We greet you with shout and with song !

DE PROFUNDIS.

AFTER A DEFEAT.

AH, God! shall tears poured out like
    rain,
  And deathly pangs, and praying breath,
  And faith as deep and strong as death,
Be given — and all in vain?

Thou claimest martyrs, — they are given, —
  What shall the stern demand suffice?
  From out our darkened homes arise
Strong cries that startle Heaven.

We murmur not, enduring all
  With broken hearts but silent lips;
  With all our glories in eclipse,
And some beyond recall.

We stand beside our dead, our eyes
   In patient sufferance raised to Thee,
   And kiss the still brows reverently, —
Behold our sacrifice!

Behold our sacrifice! We give
   The best blood of a suffering land!
   A nation's heart by its own hand
Is stricken — that Right may live!

No failure this! God's own right hand
   A victory shall write it down!
   The years shall strengthen its renown;
Be proud of it, O Land!

Thou Christ! The Godhood of thy brow
   Paled 'neath the throes of mortal pain;
   But all thy glory glows again,
Thrice-haloed, round thee now!

Give us the martyr's steadfast power,
   So, passing our Gethsemane,
   Our glory shall but brighter be
For this, our trial hour!

FOR THE STRICKEN.

IN MEMORIAM.

O WISTFUL eyes! that will not cease
 From gazing sadly after one
Who went out in the dark alone,
Although ye say, " He is at peace! "

O hearts! that will not turn away,
 But questioning stand without the door;
 He passeth through it never more,
For he hath reached the perfect day!

Even when we thought him most our own,
 His crown was nearest to his brow;
 And he redeemed his early vow,
And passed, with all his armor on.

He turned to clasp a shadowy hand,
 Unreal to our duller eyes ;
 He saw the gleams of Paradise
Break through the darkness of the land.

His gain exceedeth all our loss ;
 We linger on these barren sands, —
 He is a dweller in the lands
Bequeathed the soldiers of the cross !

THE STORY OF SUMTER.

THEN.

OVER sea and over city slowly crept the
    sullen morn,
  All the splendor of its dawning by a grow-
    ing shadow curst;
And the sunless sky that sphered us nursed
    a tempest yet unborn,
  But we waited on the Battery* for another
    storm to burst.
Grim, defiant, as some olden warrior clad in
    chilly mail,
  Sullen, signless silence brooding o'er its
    weather-beaten face,
From its brow the vapor rifted by the fresh-
    ening eastern gale,

* The battery of Charleston harbor.

Saw we Sumter, as the grayness of the
morning waned apace.
Ha! the sluggish day is shaken from its stillness by a growl,
The defiance of the Southron — spoken
from the cannon's mouth —
Blazes out the fiery ruin from beneath its
smoky cowl,
And within the walls of Sumter falls the
gauntlet of the South!
No response unto the challenge!   Are they
powerless to defy?
But what flutters from the ramparts as the
vapor parts away?
Still their own insulted colors o'er the dauntless heroes fly,
Flaunting all their braided splendors in the
sullen face of day!
Ah! behind those silent bulwarks, rising
grimly from the sea,
Waiting for the stealthy coming of the
death-dispensing shell,

There's a band of fearless spirits; guess
    how many strong they be, —
  They who stood so long and bravely, ere
    their glorious banner fell!
Seventy men to man the ramparts and to
    work each giant gun!
  Only these to face the Southrons, who are
    seven thousand strong!
Bravely toiled they from the dawning to the
    setting of the sun, —
  Bursting shell and shot around them in a
    ceaseless fiery throng!
Fast and faster belched the ruin from the
    sulphurous, yawning jaws
  Of the seven Southern batteries, armed
    and ready for the work;
All the day and all the night long well were
    plied their greedy maws,
  And until the second morning broke dis-
    consolate and murk.
Fire within and foes without them! Yet
    they struggled long and well,

From beneath their blazing shelter holding
    out against a host,
Ere the colors of the loyal from the crest of
    Sumter fell,
    And the gallant Seventy slowly left their
      well-defended post!

April, 1861.

NOW.

Now the tender budding greenery brightens
    all the earth again,
    But the sprouting grass is reddened with
      the angry bloom of war!
By the hearthstones of the nation only sounds
    the wail of pain,
    While our hero soldiers struggle in the glo-
      rious fight afar.
Thy Nemesis, O Sumter! was the thrill that
    shook the land;
    When the tidings of thy spoiling brought
      the nation to its feet,
Then was clenched, with stern intention, in-
    jured Loyalty's right hand;

Its insulted front was lifted proudly up the
    taunt to meet!

Murmur not in doubt, my brothers, at this
    trial rite of blood, —

At this purging out of error from the arte-
    ries of the land!

Never yet the walls of Treason the assault
    of Right withstood;

Ere another year hath circled ye shall
    prove it where ye stand!

APRIL, 1864.

WATCH-NIGHT.

DID I frighten you, mother, — so white
    and cold,
  And so silently here at your bed?
I could not sleep on this terrible night,
  For the battle of which we read.
To think of the dead lying out in this rain,
  Not minding its dreary fall, —
Of that mad, mad fight on the side of the
    hill;
  And he — he was in it all!

They say he was foremost in every charge,
  Till the hardiest held their breath,
Or paused in the struggle to raise a cheer
  For the man who was quits with death!
They say he was quiet and just the same, --
  No paler when acting his part;

But I know, I know how he went away,
  Stabbed even to the inmost heart.

But the fiercest pain for a tender soul
  Is doubt and its jealous pride ;
Though we do not die when we suffer so,
  Till the faithful are justified.
I tore his ring from my worthless hand,
  Denying my name of wife ;
But I wear him yet in my heart of hearts,
  And I love him with all my life.

I must go to him !   I shall never rest
  Till I falter before his feet ;
And there I shall die if he raise me not,
  And cure me with kisses sweet !
I shall die ! I shall die if I may not look
  Once more in my hero's eyes,
And see the fire of the olden love
  In their passionate deeps arise !

I have wronged his truth, I have wronged his
      love,
  And all for a whispered lie !

I have sent him to wander in search of death.
  Ah, mother, if he should die !
I will suffer all ; I deserve it all !
  But, mother, I 'm mad to go,
And beg him to take me back again,
  For I love him — I love him so !

THE LEGEND OF OUR VICTORIES

IN '61-'62.

WHAT, ho! ye valiant wrestlers!
 Ye soldiers of the Right!
Full armed by Truth and Justice
 To battle lawless Might.
Ho! I have glorious tidings!
 Come, list the tale I tell,
How the cause of UNION triumphed,
 And the crest of Treason fell.

Too long this fair young kingdom,
 The Empire of the West,
Had borne a blasting stigma
 Upon her virgin breast!
Too long the brazen foreheads
 Of a many-headed Wrong

3

Were lifted up in triumph
  Above a murmuring throng!

And the leal heart of the patriot
  Was heavy for our shame;
And we trembled for the glory
  Of our country's growing fame;
But a noble-hearted pity
  Held back the righteous blow,
For, alas! we knew a brother
  In the face of every foe.

Our wise men, looking Southward,
  Beheld the coming storm;
It had gathered, it had ripened,
  While they sounded the alarm.
The pestilence grew fouler,
  And no comfort blessed our eyes,
For the fiend that sowed this discord
  Had flouted all disguise.

We all remember SUMTER,
  And the battle's growing hum, —

How the noise of tinkling cymbals
    Was deadened by the drum.
MANASSAS stands a warning
    To our Future from our Past;
And these skies that gleam so bluely
    At BALL'S BLUFF were overcast.

Oh! then went up to Heaven
    A strong and mingled sound:
There were curses, there were pleadings,
    And tears falling to the ground.
And twin-born Strife and Treason
    Went stalking hand in hand;
And our *friends* across the ocean
    Spied the bareness of the land.

But at last we turned upon them,
    And stood in proud array;
In the West and to the Southward
    Our thunders shook the day!
On either flank beleaguered,
    Two foes our strength divide;
But Disunion, Fraud, and Ruin
    Fell down on either side!

Bravely they worked together !
 The framers of THE LIE
That teaches we have struggled,
 And succeeded — but to die ;
That teaches our achievements
 And our growing hopes are nought ;
That laughs to scorn the maxims
 That our patriot fathers taught.

We sought to save the UNION ;
 They strove to blot the name
Of Freedom's chosen country
 From the royal scroll of fame.
We strove to save the record
 Wrought out by sacred hands ;
But they to make their birthright
 The prey of distant lands.

Ho ! planters of the South land !
 Ho ! yoemen of the North !
Ye who love our glorious Union,
 Fling its banner proudly forth !
For the dastard front of Treason
 Quails beneath this sturdy blow ;

And if we stand together,
   We shall lay the curser low !

We won't give up the Union !
   Go shout it far and wide !
Missouri's head is lifted
   Once more in queenly pride ;
And Tennessee, unfettered,
   At length may proudly stand !
Out with the hand of greeting,
   All true hearts in the land !

And farther, farther Southward,
   From " the dark and bloody ground,'
From the crimson fields of Arkansas,
   Our triumph-notes resound !
And proudly o'er the waters
   Our braided colors fly, —
That flag whose splendors gladdened
   Full many a dying eye !

Shout for the glorious Union !
   Shout for the triumph gained !

In the hour that gave it to us
　　The star of Treason waned!
Well done, stanch hearts and loyal!
　　We yet shall win the day,
And see this fell disorder
　　Pass from the land away!
Nerve! nerve! each good right arm again,
　　And forward for the RIGHT!
And UNION's stainless banner
　　Shall conquer lawless Might.

THE LATEST WAR NEWS.

O PALE, pale face ! O helpless hands !
　　Sweet eyes by fruitless watching
　　　wronged ;
Yet turning ever towards the lands
　　Where War's red hosts are thronged !

She shudders when they tell the tale
　　Of some great battle fought and won ;
Her sweet child face grows old and pale,
　　Her heart falls like a stone.

She sees no conquering flag unfurled,
　　She hears no victory's brazen roar ;
But a dear face, which was her world,
　　Perchance she 'll kiss no more !

Ever there comes between her sight
　　And the glory that they rave about,
A boyish brow and eyes whose light
　　Of splendor hath gone out.

The midnight glory of his hair,
　　Where late her fingers, like a flood
Of moonlight, wandered,—lingering there,—
　　Is stiff and dank with blood!

She must not shriek, she must not moan,
　　She must not wring her quivering hands;
But sitting dumb and white, alone,
　　Be bound with viewless bands.

Because her suffering life infolds
　　Another dearer, feebler life,
In death-strong grasp her heart she holds,
　　And stills its torturing strife.

Yester eve, they say, a field was won.
　　Her eyes ask tidings of the fight;

But tell her of the dead alone
  Who lay out in the night.

In mercy tell her that *his* name
  Was not upon that fatal list ;
That not among the heaps of slain
  Dumb are the lips she 's kissed !

O poor pale child ! O woman heart !
  Its weakness triumphed o'er by strength !
Love teaching pain discipline's art,
  And conquering at length !

MITCHELL.

WRITTEN AT THE TIME OF HIS VICTORIES IN THE SOUTHWEST.

MITCHELL! strong brain, quick eye,
    and steady hand,
Faithful in service, faultless in command;
Thou favorite son of science! fit to stand
Foremost among the Saviours of the land;

In that the scholar's craft, the captain's skill,
In thee conjoined, work fitting triumphs still;
And nobler yet the patriotic thrill
Which guides the master-triumphs of thy
    will!

God! with a handful of such hearted men
To beard the wolf of Treason in his den, —

Men quick to plan and strong to act, — and
    then
Europe shall ring our triumphs back again !

Onward, my hero ! Men shall catch the
    flame
Which lights thy soul, and glow again for
    shame.
With thee, and such as thee, we shall re-
    claim
The morning glory of our empire's fame !

THE FALL OF LEXINGTON, MISSOURI.

[On this occasion the Rebels tore down the Federal flag, and
trampled it in the dust.]

A ND what though the crest of a brazen
revolt
  Is reared for the moment in insolent joy
O'er the sanctified front of our glorious
    cause,
    Whose hope and existence ye hope to de-
      stroy?

The banner whose folds ye have trailed in
    the dust
  Is sacred in spite of your dastardly hands;
And the tale of your cowardly deed shall be
    told
    With hisses and sneers in the uttermost
      lands.

In sooth, 't was a valiant and soldierly act,
  Befitting the spirits that marshal your clan,
To insult the old banner, whose folds were
    your shield,
  That looked on the hour when your glory
    began.

That flag is the type and ally of each
    deed
  That gives you a right to be proud of the
    past ;
And with it ye lay your inheritance down,
  And barter its worth for a shame that shall
    last.

But the scorn that ye cast on your glorious
    dead
  Shall arise from the ground that is rich
    with the blood
That poured, for your craven and cowardly
    sakes,
  For years in a holy and martyr-like flood.

Think ye that the parricide's labor shall
    thrive ?
  Think ye that the brow of a Cain shall be
    blessed,
When full in the eyes of a shuddering world
  He stands with the red sign of slaughter
    confessed ?

The nations shall rise in a verdict sublime ;
  The voice of their protest shall sever the
    skies ;
And the pride-stiffened neck of Rebellion
    shall bow,
  And the fire of contempt blast its insolent
    eyes !

Then shout o'er the fall of that glorious flag,
  Exult in your shame, ere its punishment
    lowers.
Your children shall blush when they tell of
    the day
  When you triumphed, but knew that the
    glory was ours !

COME WE TO THIS?

[The Rebels have discarded the good old National Air of
"Yankee Doodle," adopting "Dixie" in its stead.]

WHAT matter if its martial strains
    Record the triumph-breathing story
Of early Freedom's well-fought plains,
    And valor crowned with bays of glory?
What matter if its sound alone
    Sufficed to fire the patriot's bosom,
And with each spirit-stirring tone
    Exultant hopes sprang into blossom?

What matter if its memory 's twined
    About our costliest heritages,
And if in casting it behind
    We blur our country's proudest pages?
What matter if its tones were dear
    Unto the lion heart, undaunted,

Of him whose fame is far and near,
    Where'er our country's name is vaunted?

What matter ?   Has each freeborn soul
    Become so strangely tame and craven,
Despite the floods of noble blood
    In which its native seed was laven,
That we can brook the dastard heel
    Of Treason on our crest of glory ?
The despot's sneer, the traitor's steel, —
    Is *this* the ending of our story ?

BAKER.

THOU lion-fronted, royal man!
 Thou of the swerveless lightning glance,
Whose thunderous eloquence outran,
 O'ertopped, the minds it did entrance;—
O man, made regal by thy might,
The many-chorded soul to smite!

The lowly path was not for thee.
 Thy mental stature towered above
The wondering eyes, upraised to see
  The man whose tone and glance could
   move
A people's heart to love or hate;
Whose touch could guide it like a fate.

The glory of his life was set
 Unto a measure high and grand;

4

The lofty anthem lingers yet
    In haunting echoes through the land ;
And, greeted with a triumph-tone,
He stood, a conqueror — alone!

He fell ; — and, lo ! a mighty wail,
    A cry, sublime in grief and strength,
Proclaimed the giant lying pale,
    His mighty power undone at length ;
And for that wondrous man and strong
Went up a nation's funeral song.

For him a high applauding tone
    Shall linger in the halls of Time.
Even as he stood, he fell — alone,
    A warrior in a strife sublime.
A nation raised his burial-stone, —
He will not sleep unsung, unknown.

OUR SACRIFICE.

[To those brave men of the Fifteenth and Twentieth Massachusetts Regiments and the California Battalion, living or
dead, who took part in the battle of Ball's Bluff, this heart-
cry is dedicated.]

WELL, the hapless day is done!
    Well, its bloody course is run!
Let a pall of blackness hide it
From the glances of the sun.

Oh! the cruel, cruel fate!
Oh! the help that came too late!
Here our first and great disaster *
Surely found its fitting mate!

Ah, the hearts that bled in vain!
Ah, the heaps of loyal slain!

        * Bull Run.

Soft, my soul ; be silent ; add not
Curses to this bitter pain.

He,* the lion-heart of all,
Holding life and safety small,
If his country's clouded honor
Might be brightened by his fall.

Oh, ye steadfast ! oh, ye brave !
Filling now one common grave ;
Lo ! the nation's bosom shrines ye
With the cause ye died to save !

Shall it, shall it be for nought
That this sacrifice was wrought ?
Ha ! the nation startles fiercely,
Burning at the craven thought !

Not until the hoary flood
That is purple with your blood,
On whose banks your scanty legions
Facing brutal slaughter stood,

* Baker.

From its ending to its source
Floweth free from Rebel force, —
Not until yon far blue mountains
Have been purged of Treason's curse, —

Will we stay the costly tide
From a bleeding nation's side ;
Blood and treasure flowing freely
In an ocean deep and wide.

For a spirit is abroad
Bright and terrible with God ;
And we mark the troubled waters
Where His burning feet have trod !

UNION FOREVER.

MEN of America, press to your standard!
    Foemen are gathering anear and afar;
Swear that your life-blood shall redden
      around it,
    Ere from its azure there vanish a star.

Look where the demon of inward dissension
    Is sowing the seeds of a terrible strife;
We who stood firm against foreign encroach-
      ment,
    Are turning our hands against Unity's life.

Shall our blood-purchased glory vanish for-
      ever?
    Oh! shall we shame the pure eye of the
      day,

With a sight of the ranks of our brotherhood
broken
Forever, and siding in hostile array ?

Oh! shall the wail of the trampled and
fettered
Go up from the uttermost ends of the
earth,
And the down-trodden heads of the millions
uplifted
At the news of our destiny's glorious birth

Droop as the star of our Unity fadeth,
And the shreds of our banner are flung on
the gale ;
While the eye of the despot shall gloat o'er
the record
That tells of our shame and our failure the
tale ?

How art thou fallen, O Daughter of Promise !
From the throne of thy lofty and virgin
estate,

When thy children are drunk with the blood
    of thy suffering,
  And traitors are ringing the knell of thy
    fate!

Yet, there's a band of the stanch and de-
    voted, —
  Men whose integrity never was bought;
Deep in their leal hearts are graven the les-
    sons
  God and the deeds of their fathers have
    taught.

Strong in the might of an inborn convic-
    tion,
  Only for GOD AND THE UNION we fight,
Only to foil the designs of the traitor,
  Only to vindicate GOD AND THE RIGHT!

Union forever! our God-given motto;
  Union forever! our voices proclaim;
Union forever! our women and children
  Rise and unite in defence of its fame!

Union forever ! and death to the traitor !
  Be the bright folds of our banner unrolled.
Show to the world that its stripes are eternal,
  And its stars like the stars that the heav-
    ens enfold.

Union forever !   Oh, sons of your country,
  Swell the proud anthem that rolls from the
    heart
Of our forests of pine to the sweeping prai-
    ries ;
  Union forever ! we die ere we part !

RESURGAM.

L ET the nations talk !
　　While Freedom droops, with all her
　　　colors down,
With a great cloud upon her old renown ;
　　While in the sunlight traitors dare to walk !

　　　It is the boaster's hour !
It is the time that separates from the true
Those paltering fools who have not strength
　　　to do
　　One honest deed against an evil power.

　　　For single-hearted men,
Who know no creed but Crusade for the
　　　Right,

Whom smaller interests sway not in this
      fight,
  The Cross and Thorns of Christdom come
      again.

    What time they stand
In pillory, while Ignorance may revile,
And Prejudice may sneer with bigot smile,
  And Wrong be free to strike with dastard
      hand.

    But not for long !
Is any night that waits not for its dawn ?
From any work is God's good hand with-
      drawn ?
  Is any right o'ermastered by the wrong ?

    As the Lord liveth — No !
Above the night of this most sore distress
Shall rise the healing sun of righteousness !
  The harvest is the surer, being slow !

ON THE DEAD LIST.

WILLIS CLARE is dead, they say !
    Mother read it out to-day,
But I met the words half-way.

Did I tremble ?   Did I faint ?
Did I utter any plaint ?
I was patient as a saint.

So I grappled without sign
With this master woe of mine ;
Pride can brace us more than wine.

Prudent, was I ?   Let me die !
Ah ! I cannot act a lie,
'Neath the pure night's starry eye !

Oh, to think, this summer night,
That he lies so cold and white!
He — the bravest in the fight!

And my name was on his lips
When his blue eyes met eclipse
'Neath death's icy finger-tips.

Christ in heaven! I would have died
Glad, and proud, and satisfied
For that last hour at his side!

Oh, this bitter, bitter woe!
Will the darkness never go,
And the pain that stabs me so?

I remember summer nights
On the Hudson's breezy heights,
Full of wonderful delights.

Now I watch not for his tread,
Though the stars shine overhead;
And they tell me he is dead.

I deserve this bitter woe ;
In my pride I bade him go ;
And he loved me, — loved me so !

But my heart was full of pain
As the clouds are full of rain,
Though I would not turn again !

Do you know of any grave
Which the sullen waters lave
With a dull unending wave ?

Over which the west wind weaves
Many a pall of fading leaves,
While it sobs and moans and grieves ?

Some such lonely spot unblest,
Where a guilty soul may rest,
Somewhere in the distant West ?

If such grave you ever see, —
Emblem of mute misery, —
Think, such is my heart in me !

BELLE MISSOURI.

[This song has been set to music, and universally adopted by
the Loyalists of Missouri, in opposition to "My Maryland."]

ARISE and join the patriot train,
   Belle Missouri!   My Missouri!
They should not plead and plead in vain,
   Belle Missouri!   My Missouri!
The precious blood of all thy slain
Arises from each reeking plain.
Wipe out this foul disloyal stain,
   Belle Missouri!   My Missouri!

Recall the field of Lexington,
   Belle Missouri!   My Missouri!
How Springfield blushed beneath the sun,
   Belle Missouri!   My Missouri!
And noble Lyon all undone,
His race of glory but begun,

And all thy freedom yet unwon,
    Belle Missouri!   My Missouri!

They called thee craven to the trust,
    Belle Missouri!   My Missouri!
They laid thy glory in the dust,
    Belle Missouri!   My Missouri!
The helpless prey of treason's lust,
The helpless mark of treason's thrust,
Now shall thy sword in scabbard rust?
    Belle Missouri!   My Missouri!

She thrills! her blood begins to burn!
    Belle Missouri!   My Missouri!
She's bruised and weak, but she can turn,
    Belle Missouri!   My Missouri!
Lo! on her forehead pale and stern,
A sign to make the traitors mourn,
Now for thy wounds a swift return,
    Belle Missouri!   My Missouri!

Stretch out thy thousand loyal hands,
    Belle Missouri!   My Missouri!

Send out thy thousand loyal bands,
  Belle Missouri!   My Missouri!
To where the flag of Union stands,
Alone, upon the blood-wet sands,
A beacon unto distant lands,
  Belle Missouri!   My Missouri!

Up with the loyal Stripes and Stars,
  Belle Missouri!   My Missouri!
Down with the traitor Stars and Bars,
  Belle Missouri!   My Missouri!
Now, by the crimson crest of Mars,
And Liberty's appealing scars,
We'll lay the demon of these wars,
  Belle Missouri!   My Missouri!

5

DOUGLAS.

STOUT wrestler for the trampled Right!
  Good warrior in the desperate fight!
Strong champion of the Nation's cause!
Steel-true defender of her laws!

Oh, well for thee, the friendly clod —
Full six good feet of Western sod —
Should come between those honest eyes
And the foul deeds that here arise!

Well for the head that sleeps so low,
Unhumbled by the perjured foe;
Well for the lips that dared to speak
The truth that paled the traitor's cheek!

Oh, well that they are mute to-day,
When bigot fury holds its sway;

When Justice lays its front in dust,
And Might usurps its sacred trust !

Well that the patriot's ear hears not
The curse of those by Power forgot !
Gaunt suffering, pleading for surcease,
Whose crying is a prayer for peace !

In that thou died'st with sword unbroken,
With cheek unstained by shame's hot token ;
In that thou wert not like to them,
Who, seeing that they could not stem

This storm of Evil, Hate, and Wrong,
Bowed tamely with the cowering throng ; —
Thanks ! that the veteran's brightening fame
Was saved this deep and damning shame !

Thanks ! that his sturdy strength, unbowed,
Went out unshamed, unshorn, uncowed !
That, seeing wrongs he could not mend,
And brutish errors without end,

His keen and comprehensive brain
Was lashed to madness by such pain ; —
So, falling with his harness on,
We are but glad that he is gone.
Thy sorrows will not haunt him in his grave,
O land, for which he died, but could **not**
      save !

THE SNOW IN OCTOBER.

THE snow is falling abroad,
   Over meadow and moor ;
Drifting silently, high and white,
   O'er the sill of our cottage door.

It falls on a lonely grave
   Lying away to the West,
Where a hero heart is mouldering away, —
   The heart that loved me best !

I think of the closed blue eyes,
   And the beautiful shining hair ;
And the fresh snow heaped o'er one beloved,
   Alone in the darkness there !

The aster's heroic bloom
   And the maple's scarlet wreath

Are crushed alike by t'   hand
   Of this terrible icy (.

Oh, cruel, untimely snow !
   You have found him where he
It was too early to fold your shrou
   Over my soldier's eyes.

I could bear to leave him alone
   With the sweet south wind and the flowers,
But not with the snow and the blighted
     leaves
   Of these desolate autumn hours !

. Oh ! then I could think no more,
   And the pent-up grief grew wild,
And I bowed my throbbing, aching head,
   And wept like a weary child !

And I said, " The world is cold,
   And terribly lone and wide ;
How can I walk its dreary way,
   With no stay but my woman's pride ?

" I shall pass by cheerful homes
 Which Love hath made so bright,
But I may not stay; I must walk alone
 In the darkness and the night!

" Moan, moan aloud,
 O desolate heart of mine!
But spoken words can never give vent
 To an agony like to thine."

The snow is falling abroad,
 Silently, soft and slow,
But the tears that rain from despairing eyes
 Fall faster than the snow!

*   *   *   *   *   *   *

I watched it through my tears,
 Till the grief-throbs grew less sharp;
And I thought of a gleaming, golden crown,
 And a sweetly sounding harp!

I thought of the Great White Throne,
 And the shining robes they wear;

And the perfect peace of the purified ones,
   And the glory reigning there !

   *   *   *   *   *   *   *

The snow is falling abroad,
   Tenderly, soft and slow ;
And the quiet throbs of my heart keep time
   To the musical fall of the snow !

TO A HERO, WITH A SWORD.

(McCLELLAN. IN 1861.)

TAKE it! from a woman's hand:
   Draw it! for a suffering land:
Sheathe it only when we stand
      Shouting victory!

Childhood's lisp and woman's tears,
Pulse of pride, affection's fears,
Heart of youth and strength of years,
      Blend in this appeal.

And though we, who bid thee go,
May not with thee breast the foe,
Tears as dear as blood shall flow,
      Champion of our homes!

Lo ! our clinging hands untwine,
And no longer fetter thine ;
For our land we all resign, —
    So, we let thee go !

Take it ! decked by woman's skill, —
She whose gentle min'stries still
In the hour of trial fill
    Sterner souls with calm !

Take it ! from a woman's hand :
Draw it ! for a suffering land :
Sheathe it only when we stand
    Shouting victory !

TO A PATRIOT.

FRIEND! In this fearful struggle for the
    Right,
Oh, brother-wrestler in our common cause !
Upholder of our rudely trampled laws !
Good soldier in the fight !

I stretch to thee a not unworthy hand,
In that my soul is large enough to know
And feel the mighty truths which nerve
    thee so
To battle for our land !

I give thee greeting through my rising tears ;
I say, God speed thee on thy venturous way !
I say, if we should win this desperate day,
Through the thick-coming years

A voice shall utter how thy strength went
    forth
To nerve thine upright heart, thine honest
    hand, —
Thou, noblest of the brothers of our band,
The heroes of the North !

VICKSBURG.

VICTORY! Victory!
   The resurrected Right shall stand,
A tower of strength unto the land.
And when our spirits faint and fail,
And long endeavors leave us pale,
Across the lists of death shall flash
That memory of rare renown, —
How for so many days and nights
We lay around the 'leaguered town.
      Victory! Victory!

No transient, momentary gleam,
As fitful as a fever dream ; —
The grand fruition of a work
Cemented into moveless strength
With loyal blood and loyal breath,

And triumphing o'er Wrong at length.
    Victory!   Victory!

    Sure and slow!   Sure and slow!
While the seasons came and went,
The iron man of swerveless thought *
Planned and wrought! Planned and wrought!
The waiting spring burst into bloom,
Nor saw the fated city's doom;
Midsummer's breath was on the air,
Before suspense was broken there.
    Sure and slow!   Sure and slow!

    Victory!   Victory!
Our triumph shook the very air!
One loyal, universal shout,
In which the Nation's heart went out;
For Wrong was down, and Right was up,
And exultation everywhere.
    Victory!   Victory!

      * Grant.

LOYALTY'S LAST EFFORT.

[He did not speak or move after receiving the fatal wound,
until a comrade, bending over him, said, "What cheer for
the Union?"]

LIFE'S sands were ebbing fast,
    And darkness wrapped his failing mind
        about;
And then in gloom, at last,
    Memory's spent lamp went out.

And thus he lay,
    While slowly dragged along each weary
        hour;
Knowing not night or day,
    Suffering, bereft of power.

And Love its vigil kept, —
    Love, whose heroic spirit faltereth not!

And one, his dearest, there in anguish wept,
Because she was forgot.

Dear hands were on his brow,
True eyes in anxious pity sought his own :
" Dearest ! dost thou not know *me* now ? "
Alas ! he knew not one !

Another came,
Grasping his poor worn hand with cheering
tone :
" Knowest thou not *me ?* "   The silence was
the same ;
He groped in gloom alone.

" One question more, —
Hath no last prayer for Freedom's death-
less cause ?
O patriot heart, so bravely stanch of yore ! "
They bent in breathless pause.

And then, oh, then !
It seemed as if a blaze of glory bright

Had cleft the quickly gathering gloom in
    twain,
  And swept away the night.

The dull eye gleamed,
  The inane face was lighted up with joy;
O'er all a grand celestial radiance beamed,
  Which death could not destroy:

"God save the trampled Right!
  God keep aloft our glorious Stripes and
    Stars!
UNION FOREVER!   Comrades, to the fight!"
  Ended were all his wars.

6

AN APPEAL

IN FAVOR OF A GRAND MISSISSIPPI VALLEY SANITARY
FAIR.

[Read before the General Assembly of the loyal men and
women of St. Louis, convened at the Mercantile Library,
February 1, 1864, by Professor Amasa McCoy, of Washington, D. C.]

WHERE the Mississippi's darkly troubled
    waters
  Roll their tawny waves along;
And the South land's ever warm, but wilful
    daughters
  Change to sighing all their song;
Far away from any help or friendly sooth-
    ing,
  They are dying, day by day, —

Without love or any tender hand for smooth-
      ing
  The last frown of death away!

Who are dying? *Who* are falling in their
      places,
  Stabbed by pestilence and want;
With a firm resolve upon their pallid faces,
  Which Death can never daunt?
Who are tracking from the West land to the
      South land
  A free passage in their blood?
Who have never turned their failing footsteps
      homeward,
  Nor faltered where they stood?

Loyal men, who make the sinews of this
      nation,
  Who keep alive the throbbings of its
      heart!
Royal heroes! without thought of rank or
      station,
  By the God of battles called and set
      apart!

The champions of this crucified Republic,
　　The flower and the glory of the land!
And shall no help nor any sign of greeting
　　Go to cheer them where they stand?

In hospitals and in camps, so thickly crowded,
　　They are suffering life away,
With no blessed touch of Home to balm and
　　　　soften
　　The pain which maketh gray!
Oh, ye daughters! Oh, ye sisters! Oh,
　　　　ye mothers!
　　Are ye haunted by their eyes? —
The weary, dying looks of sons and brothers,
　　Who shall never more arise!

Let us help them! We, who sit in careless
　　　　comfort,
　　In our happy, cheerful homes, —
Shall we leave our brave defenders pining,
　　　　dying,
　　For the help that never comes?
Oh! remember that the quiet of each hearth-
　　　　stone

Is purchased with their blood ;
And for us they wear the cross and thorns
    of Christhood
In their noble martyr mood !

Let us help them ! Oh, ye hearts of loyal
    women !
  For your hands is *not* the sword !
To heal and not to wound, your blessed mis-
    sion,
  Handmaidens of the Lord !
Be the Marys of this suffering Republic ;
  Take your places at its feet ;
Ye are gentle, and your hands have skill in
    healing,
  And your words are pure and sweet !

Ye loyal men, who love the Nation's wel-
    fare,
  Help us freely, without thought ;
Strengthen well the hands by which this fear-
    ful ransom
  For Freedom's cause is wrought.

Oh, loyal hearts ! behold your country's
    altar
  Awaits your sacrifice ;
Through your offerings, the pledge of its
    redemption,
Shall its new-born glory rise !

TRUTH IS INVINCIBLE.

(VERITAS VINCIT.)

[Motto on the banner presented to a Regiment.]

VERITAS VINCIT! Our soul-stirring
    motto!
  All worthy to wave o'er the breadth of the
    world;
The banner that bears it aloft is victorious,
  And never in sorrow or shame shall be
    furled.

Veritas Vincit! Our God-given promise!
  Before it the forehead of evil must quail;
Though wrong may enshroud it, and guilt
    may becloud it, —
  A God is its author, it never can fail!

Veritas Vincit !   In triumph proclaim it !
  O knight of the holy, the pure, and the
    true !
O warrior ! O poet ! O Christian ! O states-
    man !
  O friend of the right ! here 's a motto for
    you !

Veritas Vincit ! There 's life in its music !
  Be it blazoned in glory on every true
    breast ;
And leal hearts respond to its magical ac-
    cents,
  From the North to the South, from the
    East to the West !

RANKED HIGHER.

HE fell as a soldier should fall, —
  He died as a hero should die, —
With his sword in his hand, and his face to
    the foe,
  And the victory-flash in his eye!
And proudly, in spite of its pain,
  Swells the patriot's spirit for him;
For the bays that we lay on this passionless
    brow
  No frost of the Future shall dim.

He left us, too early, alas!
  The valiant of heart and of hand;
But the tears of the pure and the blood of
    the brave
  Must flow for the life of the land.

And say, shall the poisonous root
   Of Treason e'er thrive in the soil
Now red with the blood of our princeliest
      hearts,
   And rich with our treasure and toil ?

   Ye sons of your country, awake !
   Take the path that your heroes have trod !
Your noblest and dearest have given their
      lives, —
   Owe ye nothing to right and to God ?
If your martyred are dear to your hearts,
   Let them live in the blows ye shall deal ;
Pledge remembrance of those * on the hilt of
      the sword,
   Whose hearts were as true as its steel.

      * The martyrs of Fredericksburg.

THE SNOW AT FREDERICKSBURG.

DRIFT over the slopes of the sunrise land,
  O wonderful, wonderful snow !
Oh, pure as the breast of a virgin saint !
  Drift tenderly, soft, and slow,
Over the slopes of the sunrise land,
  And into the haunted dells
Of the forests of pine, where the sobbing
      winds
  Are tuning their memory bells ; —

Into the forests of sighing pines,
  And over those yellow slopes
That seem but the work of the cleaving
      plough,
  But cover so many hopes !
They are many indeed, and straightly made,
  Not shapen with loving care ;

But the souls let out and the broken blades
  May never be counted here!

Fall over those lonely hero graves,
  O delicate-dropping snow!
Like the blessing of God's unfaltering love
  On the warrior heads below;
Like the tender sigh of a mother's soul,
  As she waiteth and watcheth for one
Who will never come back from the sunrise
    land
  When this terrible war is done.

And here, where lieth the high of heart,
  Drift, white as the bridal veil
That will never be worn by the drooping girl
  Who sitteth afar, so pale.
Fall, fast as the tears of the suffering wife,
  Who stretcheth despairing hands
Out to the blood-rich battle-fields
  That crimson the eastern sands.

Fall in thy virgin tenderness,
  O delicate snow! and cover

The graves of our heroes, sanctified,
    Husband, and son, and lover.
Drift tenderly over those yellow slopes,
    And mellow our deep distress,
And put us in mind of the shriven souls,
    And their mantles of righteousness.

THE BATTLE OF GETTYSBURG.

THE days of June were nearly done;
  The fields, with plenty overrun,
Were ripening 'neath the harvest sun,
      In fruitful Pennsylvania.

Sang birds and children, " All is well!"
When, sudden, over hill and dell,
The gloom of coming battle fell
      On peaceful Pennsylvania!

Through Maryland's historic land,
With boastful tongue and spoiling hand,
They burst — a fierce and famished band —
      Right into Pennsylvania!

In Cumberland's romantic vale
Was heard the plundered farmer's wail;

And every mother's cheek was pale,
      In blooming Pennsylvania !

With taunt and jeer, and shout and song,
Through rustic towns they passed along,
A confident and braggart throng,
      Through frightened Pennsylvania !

The tidings startled hill and glen ;
Up sprang our hardy Northern men,
And there was speedy travel then,
      All into Pennsylvania !

The foe laughed out in open scorn,
For Union men were coward-born !
And then — they wanted all the corn
      That grew in Pennsylvania !

*   *   *   *   *   *   *

It was the languid hour of noon,
When all the birds were out of tune,
And Nature in a sultry swoon,
      In pleasant Pennsylvania, —

When, sudden o'er the slumbering plain,
Red flashed the battle's fiery rain,
The volleying cannon shook again
   The hills of Pennsylvania!

Beneath that curse of iron hail,
That threshed the plain with flashing flail,
Well might the stoutest soldier quail
   In echoing Pennsylvania!

Then, like a sudden summer rain,
Storm-driven o'er the darkened plain,
They burst upon our ranks amain,
   In startled Pennsylvania!

We felt the old, ancestral thrill,
From sire to son transmitted still,
And fought for Freedom with a will,
   In pleasant Pennsylvania!

The breathless shock, — the maddened toil, —
The sudden clinch, — the sharp recoil, —

And we were masters of the soil,
     In bloody Pennsylvania!

To westward fell the beaten foe ;
The growl of battle, hoarse and low,
Was heard anon, but dying slow,
     In ransomed Pennsylvania!

Sou'westward, with the sinking sun,
The cloud of battle, dense and dun,
Flashed into fire, — and all was won
     In joyful Pennsylvania!

But ah, the heaps of loyal slain !
The bloody toil ! the bitter pain !
For those who shall not stand again
     In pleasant Pennsylvania!

Back through the verdant valley lands,
Fast fled the foe, in frightened bands,
With broken swords and empty hands,
     Out of Pennsylvania!

7

THE GRAVES OF GETTYSBURG.

[National Cemetery at Gettysburg.]

LET us lay them where they fell,
   When their work was done so well !
Dumb and stricken, — leaving others
All the glorious news to tell.

All the yellow harvest field,
Cursèd with a crimson yield,
'Neath the thrusting in of sickles,
As the battle waxed or reeled !

They, with faces to the foe,
Lost to pain, and peace, and woe,
Armored in the inspiration
Of the old heroic glow,

Rushing grandly unto death !
Eyes ablaze and 'bated breath, —
Second-sighted for the future, —
Here they piled the trampled heath !

Here for Liberty they stood,
Writ their records in their blood,
On the forehead of the epoch,
In a grand historic mood !

Let us lay them side by side,
In their awful martyr pride ;
They will slumber well and sweetly,
Spite of wailings far and wide.

And their story shall be told
When this Present, gray and old,
Loses each distinctive feature
In the Future's ample fold.

Well, the work was fitly done !
Well, the day was proudly won !

But, — this nook that bloomed with battle,
There 's no rarer 'neath the sun !

Let us lay them where they fell,
When their work was done so well !
In the martyr's noble silence,
Leaving us the tale to tell.

THE RANSOMED BANNER.

[Asa W. Blanchard, Sergeant-Major Nineteenth Regiment
  Indiana Volunteers, was killed at Gettysburg, Wednesday,
  July the 1st, while rescuing the colors of the company,
  (which had been left behind when the regiment was ordered
  to retreat, four color-bearers having been shot down,) and
  which he succeeded in saving.]

FOUR times the banner of the free
  Had lowered its front at Treason's will, —
Four times, victorious, from the dust
  It saw our arms triumphant still.

And every time its folds went down,
  A hero soul went up to God ;
Yet swift the fatal place was filled,
  And still our colors waved abroad.

The place was slippery with our blood,
  Where we fell, fighting for our land !

We dropped about, like withered leaves,
   And could no longer make a stand.

" Retreat ! " We, chafing at the word,
   Thrilled through and through with loyal
      shame, —
In sullen gloom we wheeled about,
   Our souls with fierce regret aflame !

When one, a noble, fair-faced boy,
   Whom Fate had nurtured for that hour, —
He ignorant of his high emprise, —
   Sprang up, full-statured, into power.

The ancient thrill of prophet flame,
   The spirit of our primal men,
Transfiguring our common clay,
   Flashed through the youthful hero then !

" Our flag ! our flag forever, boys ! "
   He tore it from the spoiler's hand ;
One moment o'er his dauntless head
   It waved, — the glory of the land !

And then ! — young martyr of the West,
  Our tears must drown the tribute-song ;
But ever shall thy memory live,
  While Right shall battle with the Wrong !

BRINGING HIM HOME!

[Col. ———, who led a charge at Pittsburg Landing, was
reported to be alive and well at the very time when his
body was being taken to his family.]

WHY, mother! What 's the matter?
　　How you stare!
Why won't you let me see the letter, too?
Why do you hide it? 'T is from Henry
　　Gray,
And so there must be news from the battle-
　　field, —
Perhaps a word of dearest Alfred, too!
He has not written, — he 's too busy now, —
My brave! my soldier! loyal lion-heart!
Forever foremost in the advancing ranks.
He was, I know, among the very first
To front the foe and drive him from his lair.

I read it in the paper yesterday, how the
    stanch Seventh
Swooped upon the foe, and backed their Col-
    onel in his brilliant charge.
And he? He was not hurt; they 're sure
    of that.
I breathed not, moved not, till I read so far;
And then I fell all quivering on my knees,
Not to pray, but weep out all my thankful-
    ness.
And then my life was shaken with the rush
Of the exultant blood that fired my face,
Because my soul stood proudly up and said:
" This hero whom his brethren honor so, —
This man on whom the nation's eyes are
    turned, —
Is mine, *my* husband ! " —
What is it, mother? Nay ! I 'll see it too !
It is not fair to jest and cheat me *now ;*
'T is pitiful, trifling with a hungry soul.
Give me the letter. Why ! how white you
    are !
No trifling now ! I *will* know what it means !

" Bringing him home ! "   Dear God ! — My
    life ! — What 's here ?
Bringing him home ! Why *should* they bring
    him home ?
Why, what 's the matter with my foolish
    head ?
There 's something snapped inside of it, I
    think.
Lies ! lies ! lies !   I don't believe it, — not a
    word of it !
They 've forged this letter just to frighten me ;
There 's some mistake, they mean another
    man.
Smile, sweet my mother ! for the love of
    Heaven,
And tell me for my life's sake I am right.

The world 's all dark, — my soul !
The day was bright a little while agone !
Well ! well ! I 'm hurt so deep I cannot feel
    the smart.
Let me lie down and hide my face somewhere,
In some dark place, and that is all I want.

No words!   No words!   You jar me when
     you speak ;
I never want to see the light again ! —
He 's *dead*, you say ?   Well, then, the world 's
     all dead ;
Let *me* be dead, too ! —

Bringing him home !   My pride ! my sweet !
     my all !
He wrote me he was coming ; and all day
I sat and listened for his homeward feet.
He said, " Sweet wife ! " one little week ago, —
His farewell kiss is warm upon my mouth ;
And now ? — *They 're bringing him home !*
Why ! there 's his letter on the table there, —
His very last ! and the tender hand that
     wrote
Will never stroke my nestling head again ;
And when I kiss him he 'll not kiss me back ;
And when I suffer he 'll not comfort me.
God ! are you just ?   You knew he was my
     all !
And so ! — *they 're bringing him home !*

I wonder if the violets are all dead, —
His eyes were like them !
Well, if their roots are planted on our graves,
They 'll blossom blue and thick, this time next
        year.
Oh, my dead soldier ! Oh, my life's one love !
I think I could have borne it better if
You 'd kissed me *only once* before you died !
Say, do you miss me, darling, up in heaven ?
I want you so, that if God lets me go,
I 'll leave the world to find you, —
I cannot wait until they " *bring you home.*"

PREACHING IN CAMP.

THE rich light
　　Fell tenderly and like a heaven-sent
　　　　blessing
Upon the prayerful, upturned faces
　　Of a great multitude.

　　The musical swell
Of song sublime pealed out its triumph glad ;
And my rapt soul went out upon the wings,
The viewless wings of melody, and left
　　This weary land,

And sought a glorious one beyond the stars,
Where life is love, and love is infinite ;
Where shadows never come to dim the light
　　Of perfect blessedness.

The music ceased,
And looking up, I saw, through lingering
        tears,
A wan, half spiritual form, — an earnest
        face,
Whose greatest beauty was its intense look
        Of self-devotedness.

He spoke, and then it seemed
As if that living mass had but *one* heart, —
One mighty quivering, throbbing heart, —
And each word pierced it through.

        And strong men cowered
Before his searching words, and every eye
Was drawn to his, and helpless hands were
        wrung,
And tears welled up unbidden, — stranger
        guests
To eyes unused to weep, and the rent heart
The mighty heart of that great multitude,
        Sent up its terrible wail.

And then at last
He stood all silent, weary, pale, and spent,
And quivering with emotion.   Not a sound
Was heard within the camp save murmured
      prayer
    And stifled sobs and groans

Until, with face serene and sanctified,
He raised his hands and said all solemnly :
    " Now, let us pray."

    A holy silence fell
Upon us then.   I know not what he said ;
I know not *how* he prayed ; I only know
I *felt* his words within my inmost soul,
And bowed in awe, for *God was very near.*

JEFFERSON DAVIS.

TRAITOR! Aye! Upon thy brow
　　Guilt's dark shades are lowering fast.
Fame! what is it to thee now?
　　All its serpent wiles are past.
　　　　Thou dost feel
　　　　O'er thee steal
Dire despair; 't will soon dissever
All life's joy from thee forever!

Traitor! Aye! What made thee so?
　　Couldst thou act this craven part,
Thus in hellish wisdom grow,
　　With no demon in thy heart?
　　　　He was there,
　　　　And each snare
Told upon thy weak resistance,
Till thy soul was past assistance.

For I cannot think a mortal,
   With God's seal upon his brow,
Thus could stand within the portal
   Of the Inferno; heavy woe
      Thou wilt lay
      On the day
When the fiend, with deep beguiling,
Brought thee o'er to hear his wiling.

Traitor! — to the noblest, dearest
   Interests of human life!
Traitor! — to the truest, nearest,
   Who stood by thee in the strife!
      All is o'er,
      Ah! no more
Life, its hues from fancy taking,
Shall seem fresh with each awaking.

And thy sin shall haunt thy slumber,
   Cankering all the joy of sleep;
And remorse shall make thee number
   Every breath with anguish deep.

In despair
Thou wouldst tear
From thy soul life's hateful fetter,
Couldst thou hope thy lot to better.

THE PRESIDENT'S PROCLAMATION

AUTHORIZING THE MUSTERING INTO SERVICE OF COL-
ORED REGIMENTS.

LIFT up the bowed, desponding head,
   O long-enduring race !
Let the meek sufferance of your eyes
   Abash the tyrant's face.

Take courage, O despairing race !
   The tides of fortune turn,
When white men take in kindly clasp
   The hand they used to spurn !

Go into battle side by side
   With men of fairer hue ;
We will not hinder by our scorn
   The work you have to do !

Despised, rejected, cast away,
　Ye are God's children yet!
And on the foreheads of your race
　His mercy-seal is set!

A GREETING FOR A NEW YEAR.

COME in ! come in !
    Thou shining messenger of God !
Untroubled yet by grief or sin,
Thy weary pilgrimage untrod.
    Thy unsunned brow is beautified,
And crowned with glory by His grace ;
    He breathes the blessing of His love
Upon thy young, unwritten face.

    Come in ! come in !
For millions of impatient hands
    Are stretched to draw the stranger in,
From sunrise unto sunset lands.
    The dusky children of the South,
With fair-haired Northmen, wait to press
    Upon thy rich unsullied mouth
The greeting of their happiness !

Come in! come in!
And let thy brows be olive bound,
  A hazel wand thy hand within,
And time thy footsteps to the sound
  Of breathing lyre, in measure sweet;
So shall these notes of ruffian war
  Die out abashed, in silence meet,
And Love become our guiding star.

Come in! come in!
And let thy song be sweet and mild;
  So, haply, hearing thou shalt win,
And calm this storm of passion wild,
  And bid this jarring discord cease,
To the grand chorus of our song
  Restore the missing voice of Peace,
And crush the many-headed Wrong!

Come in! come in!
We crown thee with our holiest prayers,
  Almost to suffering akin,
For they are breathed through suppliant tears.
  We crown thee with a reverent hand,

That gives its nearest, dearest gift, —
   A wish — that from our troubled land
Thy coming may the shadows lift !

   Come in ! come in !
We 'll pledge thee in a draught divine, —
   A rarer, costlier ne'er hath been, —
And Hope shall bear the blushing wine.
   It mantles with the high resolve
Of many a noble patriot heart,
   No matter who may traitor prove,
We trust in God and do our part !

A SUPPLICATION.

DEAR Lord! our wandering feet
  Come to Thy mercy-seat;
Oh, let Thy favor greet
  Our poor endeavor!
Turn not away Thy face,
Let not the dwelling-place
Of Thy redeeming grace
  Be void forever!

God of the fair and free!
We bring our cause to Thee,
Humbly, on bended knee,
  A suffering nation!
Oh, hear! Thou wilt and must;
Thou canst not scorn our trust,
Nor tread into the dust
  Thine own creation!

Hear us, our fathers' God!
Stay Thy chastising rod,
Our feet the ways have trod,
  Of desolation.
Lay by Thy righteous wrath,
Preserve us free from scath,
Shine o'er our onward path,
Be our salvation!

Arise! Thy people free,
Erst as on Galilee
Bid these dark discords flee,
  Thy triumph voicing.
Let all the earth arise,
With loud, exultant cries
Unite to rend the skies
  With strong rejoicing!

THE VOLUNTEER'S RETURN.

AH! you 're come back too late, darling!
  'T is but to see me die;
Trust not this strange, delusive glow,
  This brightness in my eye;
For see how lightly lies my hand,
  How thin within your clasp, —
So quick and strong its pulses were
  When last it felt your grasp!

This poor, unworthy face, darling,
  Ah! hide it in your breast;
'T is long since last my weary head
  To its true home was pressed.
I only want to lie and look
  Into your blessed eyes;
'T is weary months since thus they shone
  So free from all disguise.

And when I saw you march away,
  Without one parting word,
While the brave hearts of your regiment,
  By martial notes were stirred,
I felt the ice within my heart,
  The fire within my brain ;
And all my life since then has been
  One long-enduring pain !

Ah, God ! if I could live, darling !
  Live but for your dear sake ;
To think that I must leave you now,
  My heart is like to break !
And yet 't is not such weary pain
  As when you went away ;
Oh, I suffered and I missed you so,
  Through every dreary day !

And then 't was dreadful, when the night
  Brought back your darling face,
And gave me in a mocking dream
  Its dear, remembered grace,

To start and stretch my yearning arms
   And clasp the empty air, —
To waken in the cold and dark
   And feel you were not there !

To know that you were lost, darling,
   To me forevermore, —
To know my soul's young life had shed
   The freshness that it wore
When we walked together hand in hand,
   And I looked up to you,
To read within your eyes your thought
   Of all that I might do !

Too late, too late I found, darling,
   You were the world to me !
My highest pride, no matter what
   The careless eye might see.
But I never wronged you, even in thought, —
   My pulse's lightest beat
Was yours, even as the faithful heart
   You trampled 'neath your feet.

But now you know it all, darling,
    You know that I was true, —
They could not stir one bitter thought
    For all that they could do ;
Within your strong and tender arms
    This last time let me lie,
And tell me that you love me, dear,
    Once more before I die !

I do not mind it now, darling ;
    Here, take my hand in thine, —
You may find a brighter, fairer face,
    But ne'er a heart like mine !
Oh, hold me closer, closer yet,
    And kiss me ere we part !
I 'd rather die and keep your love,
    Than live and lose your heart !

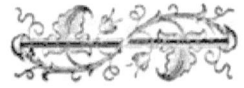

OUR CAUSE

IN 1861.

BY all the undying memories of the past,
  Which shall this hour of treacherous
      calm outlast,
We know we stand
  Above an Etna of unquenched fire,
Which, soon or late, shall burst upon the
      land
  In its resistless ire.
These gauds which deck its sod in gay array,
  Must soon be torn away, —
The awful secret from its depths come forth,
To scare the wondering earth!

  Because an evil power,
  In one unguarded hour,

Guised in the folds of Freedom's virgin vest,
Crept into a great nation's peaceful breast.
  None dreamed of inward foe ;
  And, working sure, but slow,
At length the Curse, with high uplifted head,
Defied, and sought to tread
Into the dust the friend whose heart its life
    had cherishèd !

The soul of Treason came,
And breathed with breath of flame
  On the cool waters of a nation's rest ;
And Wrong walked through the land,
With overbearing hand ;
  And from the East to the resounding
    West,
Contention's brands flared out,
And Indignation raised the mutinous shout !

A band of frantic fools,
  Gone mad upon the *isms* of the day,
Are Treason's chosen tools,
  Drawn up against us, in a rash array !

Our equals, and our brothers yet, — but late
They seek to rank above us in the State,
To wrest from us a God-donated right,
 By force of fraud or might.
Of all hope for the present now bereft,
 What course to us is left?

 But one. And yet,
 We cannot quite forget
They are co-claimants in each blood-bought
   right;
That, hand to hand to Freedom's fearless
   fight
Their sires with ours went forth, —
Though, in the oneness of their patriot worth,
They knew not of a separate South or North.

And could they live
 To view the fortunes of this desperate day,
We know that they would give
 Their blessing to our Union's Rights ar-
  ray!
The cause in which they fought,

In that our deeds are wrought.
   Our foes must understand,
   No impious human hand
May dare their sacred compact set at nought!

But they who say
   That hands of ours have lit this baleful
      fire, —
They wrong the lion at bay,
   Mistake the impulse of our righteous ire!
No! loyal hearts bleed for the wanton wreck
   That envy's hand hath made, —
To see our glorious star-crown pale and fade,
   And Treason's dastard foot on Union's
      neck;
Even tears of living blood could not atone
The grievous wrong unto our Present done!

   Be it upon the heads
   Of those who sought to tread
The interests of their brothers in the dust!
They were recreant to each sacred trust.
Our temperate pleas were thrust
   9

Back with insulting defiance to our hand ;
   We were driven to the wall, —
   We must either fight or fall, —
No choice was left us but this desperate stand.

But, brothers, we are strong,
Clad in the God-born might which doth be-
    long
To every soul that hath its quarrel just,
Not on the treacherous sand we plant our
    trust,
   But on an enduring rock,
   Which feeleth not the shock
Of each presumptuous and assaulting **Wrong.**
   God fighteth for the Right !
   He will our prayers requite,
   And lead us from this darkness to the
    light !

   Oh, we could pray that **Peace,**
   With its soft, silken ease,
Might settle down upon our troubled land,
And stay the impious hand

That would dissolve the band
That holds the jewels of our country's crown !
   But be it life or death,
   Soft words or defiant breath,
The motto of our banner gleameth bright,
Triumphant o'er the night, —
God and our life-blood for the assaulted
      Right !

IN 1864.

   Oh, triumph-bells, ring out,
   And voice the exultant shout, —
The anthemed chorus of a Nation's soul !
   The tides of battle roll
   Our Venture to its goal !
And, on the forehead of this war-worn age,
   The Angel of all time
   Shall grave a deathless rhyme ;
We pause to turn the last unwritten page,
Whose story shall each unborn race engage.

MY ABSENT SOLDIER.

EVENING shades are falling, dearest,
  Night is drawing on,
And the sweet stars look out shyly,
  Slowly, one by one ;
And I count them, with my forehead
  Pressed against the pane ;
We did it once together, dearest,
  Now I do so once again.

When I fold my hands, dearest,
  To breathe a " good-night " prayer,
Whose name is it lingers longest
  On the evening air ?
Yours.   And then I slumber softly ;
  For I know our Lord

Through the night's long hours of darkness
  Hath you in His ward!

How much I think of you, dearest!
  I know that very oft
My features rise before you,
  And then your voice grows soft;
They do not know the reason
  It thrills and trembles so;
'T is the beautiful heart-music
  That makes it sweet and low!

God bless you! my own darling,
  And keep you pure and fair;
May the calm glory of your eyes
  Be darkened by no care;
Your love, the dearest next to God's,—
  Your worth, my highest pride:
Sweet angels guard your homeward path,
  And haste you to my side!

But if—ah, God! the bitter thought!—
  You should not come again,—

If you should lie out, cold and still,
    Among the battle's slain, —
I could not bear such anguish, love,
    For all that I could do ;
I know my widowed heart would break,
    And I should perish too !

L. H. R.

OH, soldier-heart! Oh, knightly soul!
  Thine is the noblest skill of all, —
That keepeth strength, and blood, and brain,
  Responsive at thy country's call!

No thought of risk, no mean distrust,
  Doth mar the splendor of thy life!
Unbound by any party creed,
  Full-powered, thou goest to the strife.

Why, let them strain, the paltering crew!
  Who toil for gain, and not for Right;
True heart! true hand! thy deeds proclaim
  The man who makes the noblest fight!

MY STORY.

FEBRUARY 14, 1864.

BRAVE, generous soul! I grasp the hand
　　Which instinct teaches me is true ;
This were indeed a royal world,
　　If all were like to you!

You know my story.　In my youth
　　The hand of God fell heavily
Upon me, — and I knew my life
　　From thence must silent be.

I think my will was broken then, —
　　The proud, high spirit, tamed by pain ;
And so the griefs of later days
　　Cannot distract my brain.

But my poor life, so silence-bound,
   Reached blindly out its helpless hands,
Craving the love and tenderness
   Which every soul demands.

I learned to read in every face
   The deep emotions of the heart;
For Nature to the stricken one
   Had given this simple art.

The world of sound was not for me;
   But then I sought in friendly eyes
A soothing for my bitter loss,
   When memories would rise.

And I was happy as a child,
   If I could read a friendly thought
In the warm sunshine of a face,
   The which my trust had wrought.

*   *   *   *   *   *   *

But then, at last, they bade me hope,
   They told me all might yet be well;

Oh ! the wild war of joy and fear,
　　I have not strength to tell !

*　　*　　*　　*　　*　　*　　*

Oh, heavier fell the shadow then !
　　And thick the darkness on my brain,
When hope forever fled my heart,
　　And left me only pain.

But when we hope not we are calm,
　　And I shall learn to bear my cross,
And God, in some mysterious way,
　　Will recompense this loss.

And every throb of spirit-pain
　　Shall help to sanctify my soul, —
Shall set a brightness on my brow,
　　And harmonize my whole !

By suffering weakened, still I stand
　　In patient waiting for the peace
Which cometh on the Future's wing, —
　　I wait for God's release !

A nation's tears !   A nation's pains !
   The record of a nation's loss !
My God ! forgive me if I groan
   Beneath my lighter cross !

Henceforth, thou dear, bereavèd land !
   I keep with thee thy vigil-night ;
My prayers, my tears, are all for thee, —
   God and the deathless Right !

WAITING FOR VICTORY.

NATIONS may side with wrong;
      Right shall endure !
Justice may suffer long;
      Right shall endure !
Stubborn, and hot, and strong,
Traitors about us throng ;
This our unaltered song :
      Right shall endure!

What though they battle well?
      Right shall endure !
This be their final knell :
      Right shall endure !
Eager their lives to sell,
Heroes who grandly fell

Lingered this truth to tell:
      Right shall endure!

What though the fight be hard?
      Right shall endure!
Be the day evil-starred, —
      Right shall endure!
Triumph, at first debarred, —
Victories in dawning marred, —
Fall back upon your guard!
      Right shall endure!

Stars that are fixed may fall;
      Right shall endure!
Darkness may cover all;
      Right shall endure!
Ruin may droop its pall,
This our unshaken wall;
We, from behind it call:
      Right shall endure!

Let the world say its nay!
      Right shall endure!

Let the false have its day !
   Right shall endure !
Failure may block the way, —
Error may bring dismay, —
Fixed, through this long delay,
   Right shall endure !

CHARGE OF BLAIR'S BRIGADE AT VICKSBURG.

YE glorious few, who blenched not, look-
    ing Death
  Full in the face, with eyes of proud dis-
    dain, —
Who won a benediction from the land,
  Through such an offering of martyr pain!

Be proud, ye brave! God writes a victory
    down,
  And no defeat! — say traitors what they
    will,
To you the world awards the hero's crown,
  To them a scorning sharp enough to kill!

Oh, souls sublime from wrestling with the
      wrong !
  I, a weak woman, scarcely dare to raise
  My voice, through tears, to swell this burst
      of praise,
But that enthusiasm makes me strong !

LOST IN THE WILDERNESS.

[The Battles of the Wilderness.]

MY love! my only love!
   Where lies thy head to-night?
Oh, 't is weary waiting for break of day,
   And for tidings of the fight!

Somewhere in a crowded camp,
   Or, mayhap, on a ghastly field,
Is lying one whom my jealous heart,
   To death will never yield.

My love! my only love!
   But the rivers roll between,
And the land, it stretcheth for weary miles,
   In summer beauty green!

My love! my only love!
  But the night is long and lone,
And my heart goes out, through the dreary
      dark,
  With a sore, unsoothèd moan!

My love! my only love!
  But my arms are vacant yet,
And the cheeks that are fading, because un-
      kissed,
  With passionate tears are wet!

My love! my only love!
  My life is a wearing pain,
And its fulness of unshed tenderness
  Maketh it ache again!

My love! my only love!
  I will arise and go;
To find thee is all that is left to me,
  If thy glory lieth low.
    *   *   *   *   *   *   *
Alas! and she could not know,
  That the grass was springing green,

And the rank weeds hiding a something
    where
  A knightly soul had been.

Alas, for the faithful heart!
  Alas, for its yearning pain !
Hé hath laid him down in the Wilderness,
  Never to rise again !

BUTLER'S BLACK BRIGADE.

SO they will not fight! those branded
      men,
  Whose crime is a dusky skin;
They are dark without, so 't is fair to think
  The blood must be pale within!
They will not fight? You have crushed them
      long,
  They 've forgotten the way to turn!
They have brains, and yet they remember
      not;
  And hearts, but they never burn!

So, they will not fight? You remember how
  They cowered in last July? *

       * The New York riots, July, 1863.

They had done no wrong, but their skins
    were black,
  'T was fitting that they should die !
They did not fight, but they stand to-day,
    As stanchly as fairer men ;
They are helping you on to your triumph
    now,
    Who were hunted and tortured then !

Oh, ye will not take in a kindly clasp,
    The hand that is darker than yours !
And ye will not walk in a plainer light,
    Nor bury these ancient scores !
Oh, shame for your senseless and narrow
    creed !
    And shame for your savage hate !
And shame for the dulness that does not
    know,
    Like ever will seek its mate !

" Free," not " equal," for Mind must rule,
    And Mind must decide the caste ;
And the largest brain, though the lowest
    down,

Must go highest up, at the last.
What is it ye fear, if Mind must rule,
  And the earth is so very wide?
Oh, shame for your shortness of mental
      sight!
  And shame for your shallow pride!

So they will not fight?   But the grim old
      man *
  Will tell you another tale, —
Fort Pillow 's their St. Bartholomew!
  Sepoys of the South, grow pale!
Perhaps, when they hallow this common
      cause
  With their thousands of nameless graves,
Your selfish hearts will proclaim at last,
  They are men, and they are not slaves!

          * Butler.

TO A. E.

(IN PRISON AT RICHMOND.)

THERE is a spirit in that small, slight
    frame,
Which long captivity could never cow ;
And the eye, pent beneath that hanging brow,
Would never blench before the barèd steel.
Prisoner of Richmond ! As thou standest now
I see the prison-blight upon thy face !
How didst thou suffer, in those long, dull
    days,
And harder yet, those terrible, still nights !
No word from home ! No wifely fond em-
    brace ! *
Long years of peace can never do away
The memory of those pangs that turned the
    spirit gray !

---

* In one of the entries in his journal he says, " If I could
only hear from my wife ! "

KENTUCKY'S CRITTENDEN

IN 1861.

HE has given all!
His heart, his soul, his strength, his
manhood's prime;
Be very, very gentle with him, Time,
And let our prayers thy stern demands fore-
stall.

He has given all!
Oh, ripening head, God's harvest is anear;
Oh, gentle eyes! so ready with a tear,
At suffering's plaintive call.

He has given all!
Not vainly, — like some blessed household
word,

Whose dropping quivereth on some tender
    chord,
His name shall ever fall!

IN 1863.

He is at rest!
'T was like a lying down to peaceful dreams,
Lulled by the murmuring of summer streams,
To be awakened by the morrow's dreams.

He is at rest!
All noisy sorrow were unfitting now;
We drop no tears above this marble brow,
And to this late bereavement humbly bow.

He is at rest!
With reverent hands we bear him o'er the
    sod,
Where lately oft his trembling footsteps trod,
And leave him in this quiet with his God.

THE QUIET MAN.

(GRANT.)

THERE was no feasting when he marched
    away,
　No patriotic speeches ;
His calm belief in Right had placed him
    where
　No egotism reaches.

He was above them all, — that motley crowd,
　Enthusiasts and pretenders,
Who make long speeches, and who love to
    call
　Themselves the land's defenders !

Then he went gravely, earnestly to work,
　And lo, a great sensation !

For soon they found he was the only man,
  With skill to serve the nation.

And so they said, " Among the men who
    aspire
  To office let us rank you ; "
But he was neither fool nor knave, and said,
  Decidedly, " No, thank you."

At last they gave up trying to make him talk,
  And cheered for him immensely ;
But he held quiet, and was not satisfied,
  Unless he worked intensely.

" One still, strong man ! " We 've waited
    long for him ;
  He lives by acts, not speeches.
Legion of talkers ! do you heed the truth
  His life-endeavor teaches ?

H. T. B.

BE strong of heart, my genial, generous
    friend!
And falter not before this league of crime:
I hear the angel of the Coming Time
Cry to the nations, "This is not the end!"

I trace the patriot's self-forgetting thought
Upon a forehead where unselfish care
And noble toiling leave the marks of wear;
And generous feeling — pained or over-
    wrought.

But yet be strong! It shall not be in vain —
This wrestling through the darkest hour of
    fate,
For we shall go through Triumph's lifted
    gate
To find our solace for this night of pain!

THE LAST POEM.

O brave and gentle hero-soul!
    O spirit tender, tried, and true!
How could I close my record here,
    Without one little word for you?

Whose stronger arm has held me up,
    Whose stronger heart has strengthened
        mine,
Whose eye was always first to see
    The meaning of God's deep design!

Whose deeds were noble, first and last,
    As tale of ancient chivalry;
Whose sweet, exceeding faithfulness,
    Made life so beautiful for me!

Whose teachings filled my spirit with
   This strong, unfaltering belief,
That God's good hand will save the right,
   Through failure and bewildering grief.

Ah! no caressing hand is laid
   In commendation on my head,
My soul, dividing time and space,
   Is leaning toward yours instead!

I cannot think it vainly yearns
   To reach you, though bereaved I stand;
Though it is bitter pain to miss
   The touch of your protecting hand.

Not lost, but absent! Will you take
   These first-fruits of a younger soul?
You know how long ago God gave
   Its throbbings into your control.

THE END.